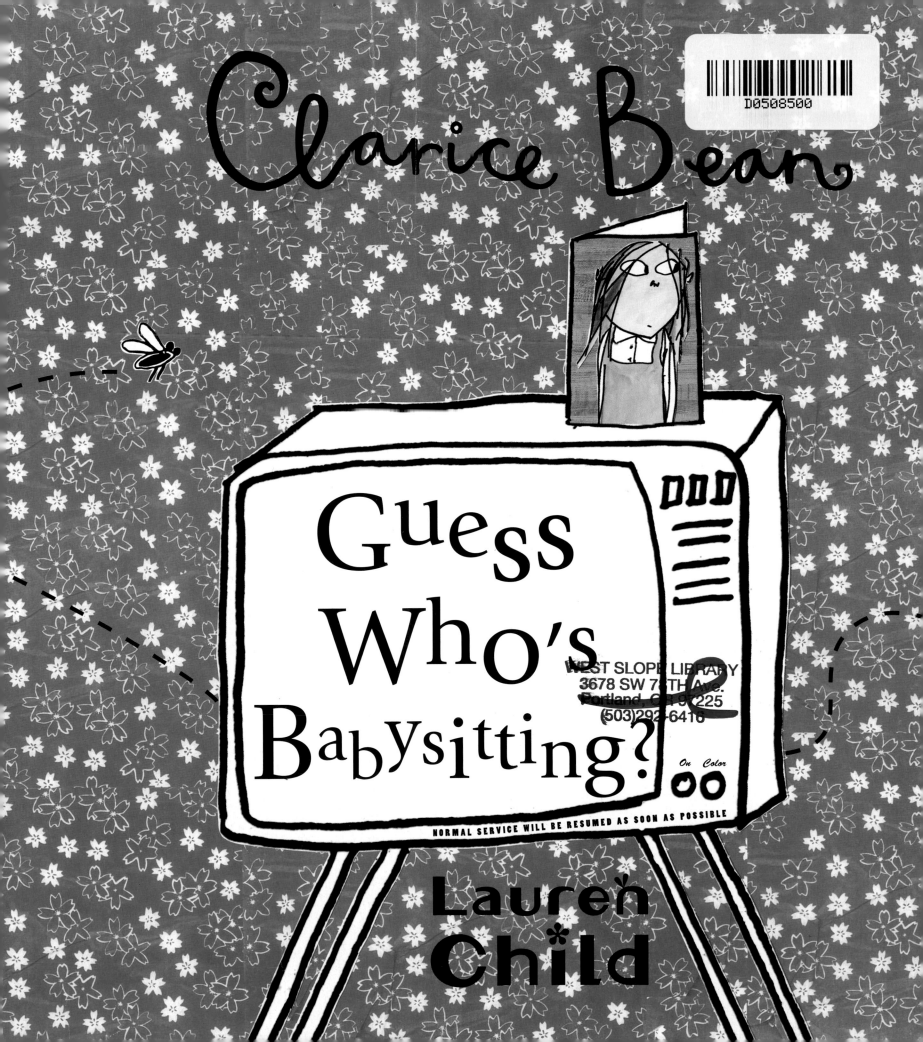

Clarice Bean

Guess Who's Babysitting?

Lauren Child

NORMAL SERVICE WILL BE RESUMED AS SOON AS POSSIBLE

On   Color

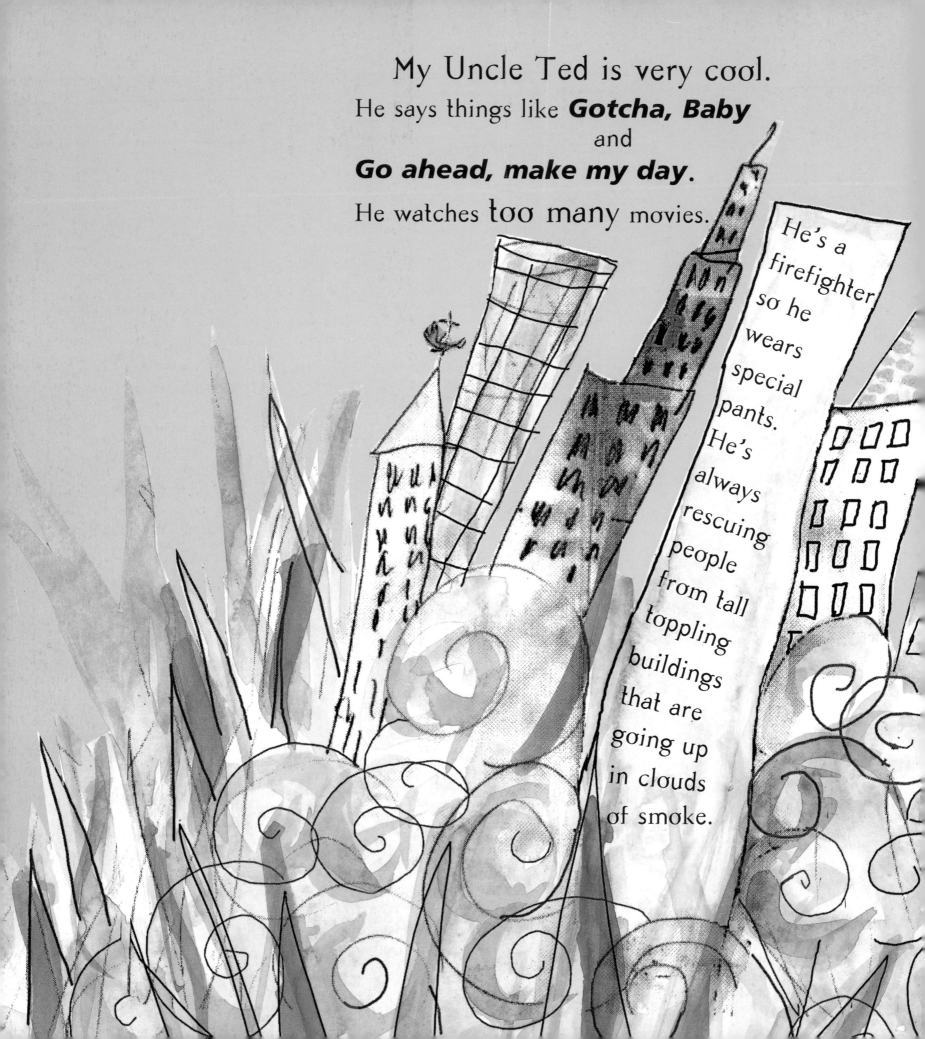

My Uncle Ted is very cool.
He says things like **Gotcha, Baby**
and
Go ahead, make my day.

He watches too many movies.

He's a firefighter so he wears special pants. He's always rescuing people from tall toppling buildings that are going up in clouds of smoke.

He can get you in a firefighter's carry
before you can say

Uncle Ted put me dOWn!

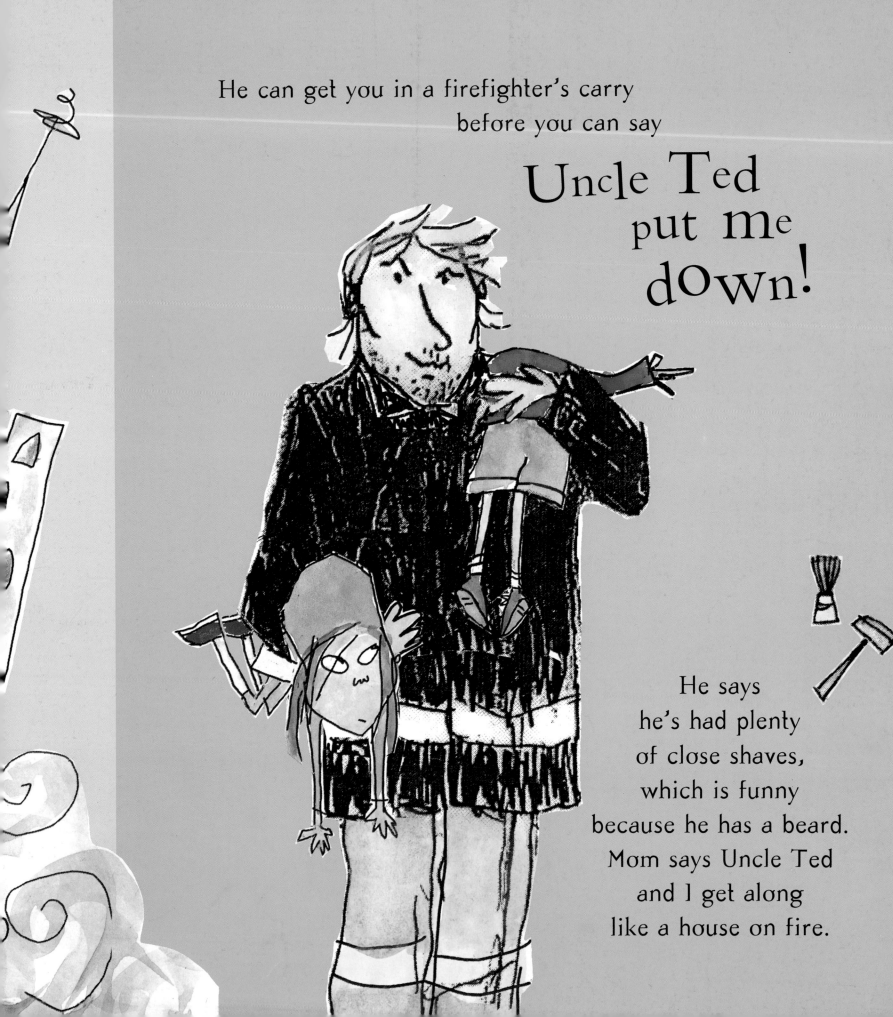

He says
he's had plenty
of close shaves,
which is funny
because he has a beard.
Mom says Uncle Ted
and I get along
like a house on fire.

This book is for my sister Rachel, who was crazy about guinea pigs, and for my sister Jenny, who preferred cars.

RACHEL

JENNY

♡ Also for my friend Lindsay Isobel Hart.

Thanks to Olga at the guinea pig rescue center

Library of Congress Cataloging-in-Publication Data is available.

Library of Congress Catalog Card Number 00–037963

First Published in Great Britain in 2000 by Orchard Books, London.

Designed by Anna-Louise Billson

ISBN 978-0-7636-4797-1

09 10 11 12 13 14 CCP 10 9 8 7 6 5 4 3 2 1

Printed in Shenzhen, Guangdong, China

Candlewick Press
99 Dover Street
Somerville, Massachusetts 02144

visit us at www.candlewick.com

This book has been printed on paper made from sustainable forest timber.

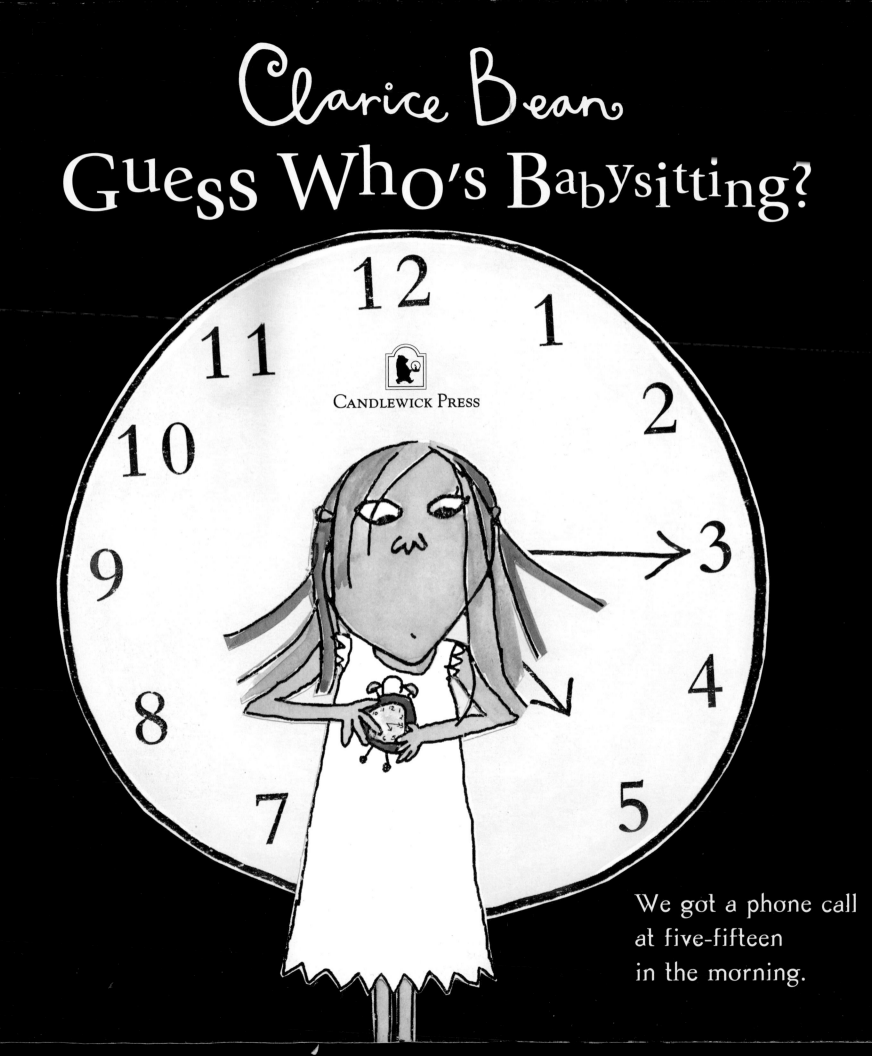

We got a phone call
at five-fifteen
in the morning.

It turned out Mom's older brother,
Uncle Ernie, *slipped* on a doughnut
getting out of his squad car.

He's a
policeman in
New York City
so he's used
to life's
ups and *downs*.

The
nurse says

could

Someone will have to babysit because
Dad is also going away, on Important Business.

Marcie (my big sister) says,
**I would rather look after newts
from Neptune than
be left with Clarice Bean (me)
and Minal Cricket**
(my little brother).

Kurt
(my big brother)
says,

**Don't look at me, I'm going
to my room and probably
won't be down for supper.**

Minal says,
What
about
Grandad?

Grandad says,
I haven't had
a doughnut
since I was
a boy.

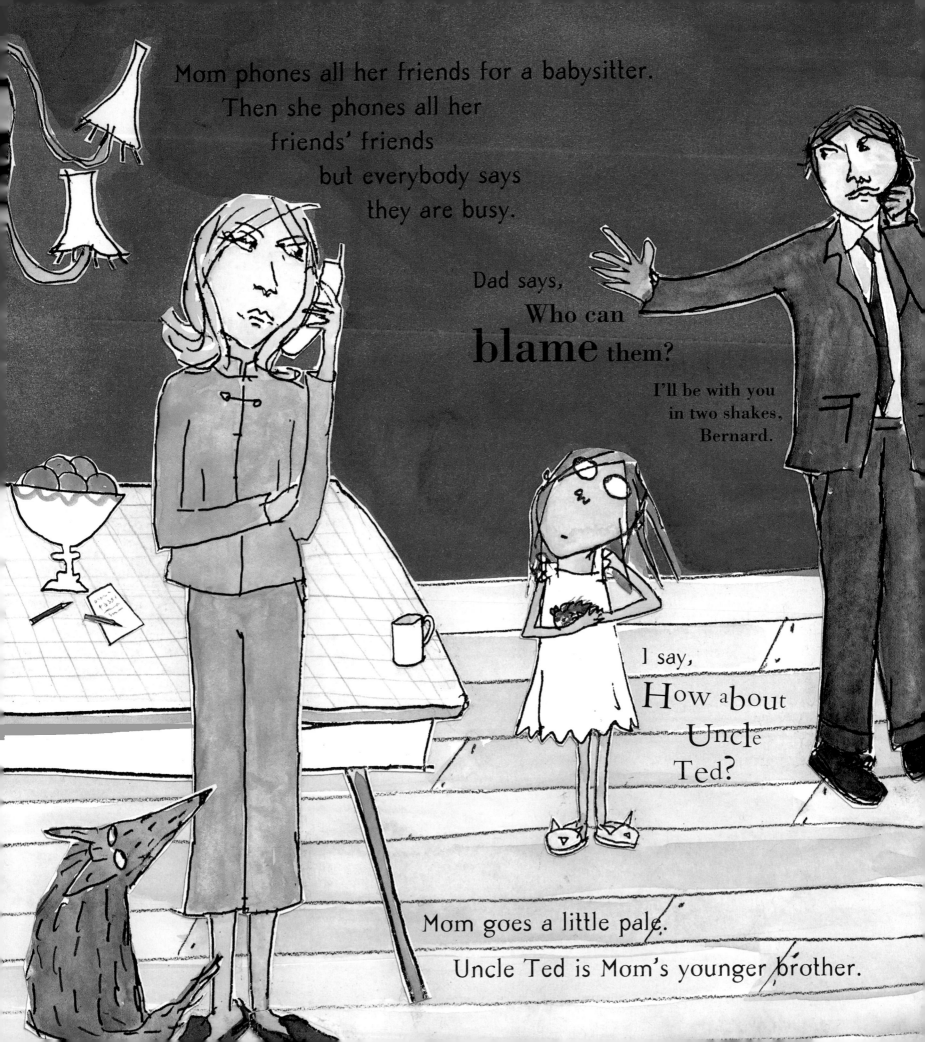

Mom phones all her friends for a babysitter.
Then she phones all her
friends' friends
but everybody says
they are busy.

Dad says,
Who can
blame them?

I'll be with you
in two shakes,
Bernard.

I say,
How about
Uncle
Ted?

Mom goes a little pale.

Uncle Ted is Mom's younger brother.

When Uncle Ted needs a break from firefighting
and cats up trees he comes over to our house.
And then
things get a little wild.

*Get off your horse
and drink your milk.*

Uncle Ted and I love to watch Westerns on the edge of our seats
with plates of eggs and beans
perched on our laps.

Uncle Ted is teaching me cowboy techniques.
One time he lassoed the lamp.

Mom said,
*I'd rather have everything in one piece
thank you very much.*

Uncle Ted looked sheepish.
I lassoed my brother.
He wasn't too happy either.

So you can see why Mom is nervous about leaving Uncle Ted in charge but it turns out she can't be so choosy. Mom gives Uncle Ted **very** strict instructions.

1. NO BREAKAGES

2. NO LASSOING

3. DON'T DRIVE MRS. STAMPNEY AT NUMBER 9 WACKO

4. MAKE SURE KURT SEES DAYLIGHT AT LEAST ONCE EVERY 24 HOURS

6. KEEP AN EYE ON GRANDAD HE TENDS TO WANDER OFF

5. DON'T LET MARCIE TAKE THE PHONE INTO HER BEDROOM

chat chat chat chat chat chat chat chat chat

Uncle Ted says,

Yes, Ma'am. I hear you loud and clear.

Everything goes **really well** for the first two days.

Nobody is arguing and we are like one of those families on television who always say things like

please

and

thank you

and

sorry . . .

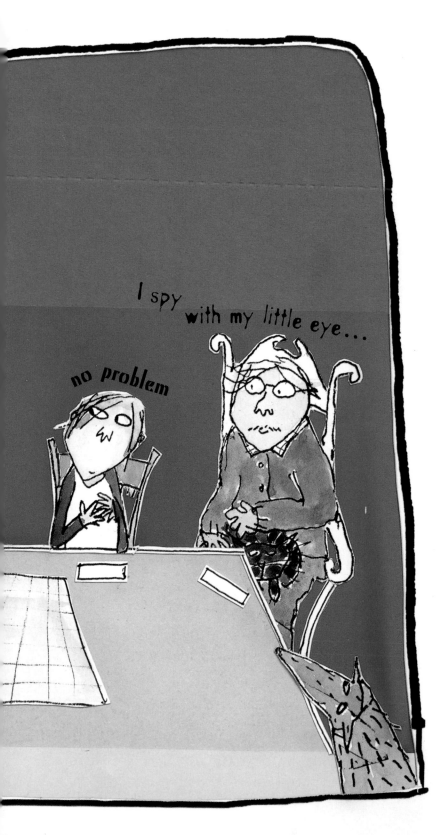

...and they let people share their stuff without grumbling.

Kurt even sits in the backyard and almost gets a tan. He never normally goes outside. He says it's too bright.

BUT THEN . . .

. . . Minal ruins everything
by taking Albert out of his hutch without asking.
I am supposed to be taking care of him over spring break.
(Albert is the school guinea pig so it's a VERY
RESPONSIBLE
JOB.)

Albert

Albert makes

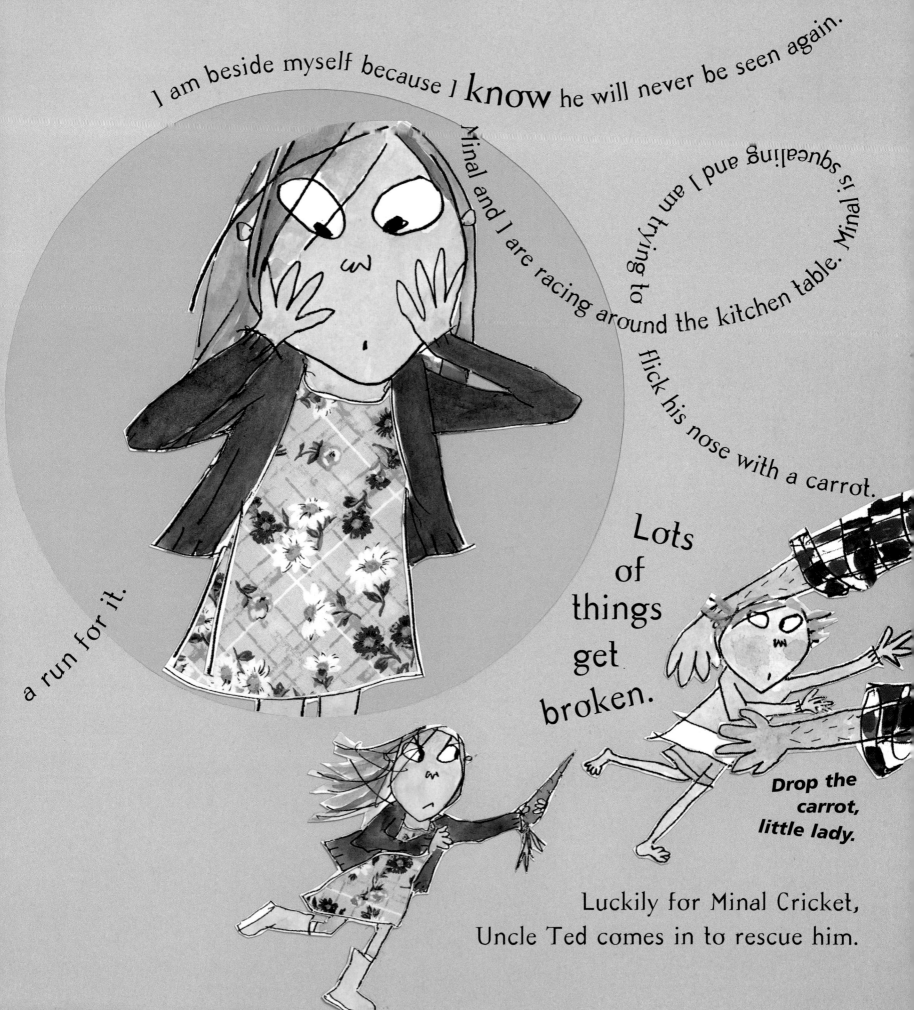

I am beside myself because I **know** he will never be seen again. Minal and I are racing around the kitchen table. Minal is squealing and I am trying to flick his nose with a carrot.

a run for it.

Lots
of
things
get
broken.

Drop the carrot, little lady.

Luckily for Minal Cricket,
Uncle Ted comes in to rescue him.

To take my mind off
the worry of
losing a guinea pig
we all go outside
and play soccer.

And it works because Uncle Ted kicks the ball so hard that it knocks Minal out.

We have to **drive** to the e m e r g e n c y r o o m at **50** miles an hour at least!

Hang on to your hats!

Minal is fine but they still give him an X-ray and a little carton of orange juice.

Minal loves it because he can show off and lie under a blanket and whimper.

I say he should have stitches but unfortunately the nurse doesn't agree.

When we get home we find Grandad is missing.
Uncle Ted phones all the neighbors
and is about to dial 911 when
Mrs. Stampney
calls to say she has found Grandad
in
her
living room.

Watching the races.

She's pretty grumpy about it.

Uncle Ted says,

How on earth did you end up here?

Grandad says,
All the houses look the same
when you get to my age.

But I know it's really because
Mrs. Stampney has a bigger TV than we do,
plus, she's got a remote control.

I'm still worried sick about Albert so I go into the yard to see if he's back in his hutch.

I had left a carrot there
to lure him
but
it's still unnibbled.

The next thing I know,
Robert Granger,
the boy next door,

pops over

the wall.

He says,
Do you want to pet **my guinea pig?**

I say, That's not your guinea pig. That's Albert.

He says, It's not Albert. **It's Belinda.**

I say,
You better give him back, Robert Granger.
That's school property and you will be in **big** trouble with the police.

Robert Granger is so nervous he lets Albert **wriggle** out of his hands.

Albert s c u t t l e s through the house

and out the front door.

Uncle Ted shouts, **After him!**

We are madly c h a s i n g the guinea pig who **charges** through the fence.

Minal squeezes after him and gets stuck like a giant squeaking tomato. I say, Lucky you are here, Uncle Ted, because you can rescue him in next to no time.

(Rescuing people from fences is normal for Uncle Ted and he doesn't look a bit worried.)

Uncle Ted says, **Hang in there, Buddy.**

He races off to call his friends at the fire station. But it takes him forever to find the phone.

chat
    chat
chat
    chat
. . . so anyway,
    I said . . .
    chat   chat
        chat
. . . and then guess
    what he said . . .

chat

chat

chat
chat
chat

In the meantime
Mom comes back from the airport.
She reaches right into her bag
for her new bottle of bubble bath
and rubs it on Minal's head.
She wriggles him free in

two minutes
flat.

Bubble
Bath

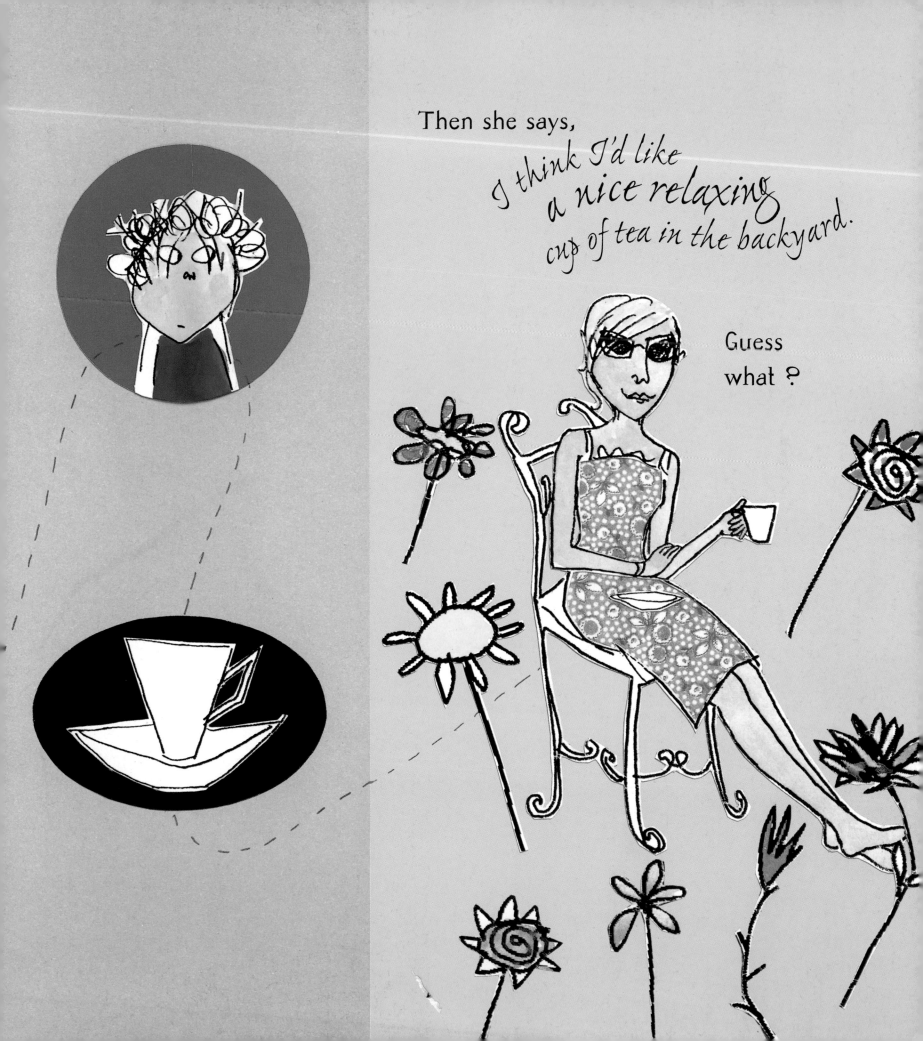

Then she says,

I think I'd like a nice relaxing cup of tea in the backyard.

Guess what?

The whole fire
department shows up.
　　Mom doesn't
look at all
　　　　surprised.
She just glares at
Uncle Ted.

Minal is
already rescued.

It turns out Uncle Ernie is feeling much better, but he doesn't think he will ever be able to look at a doughnut again.

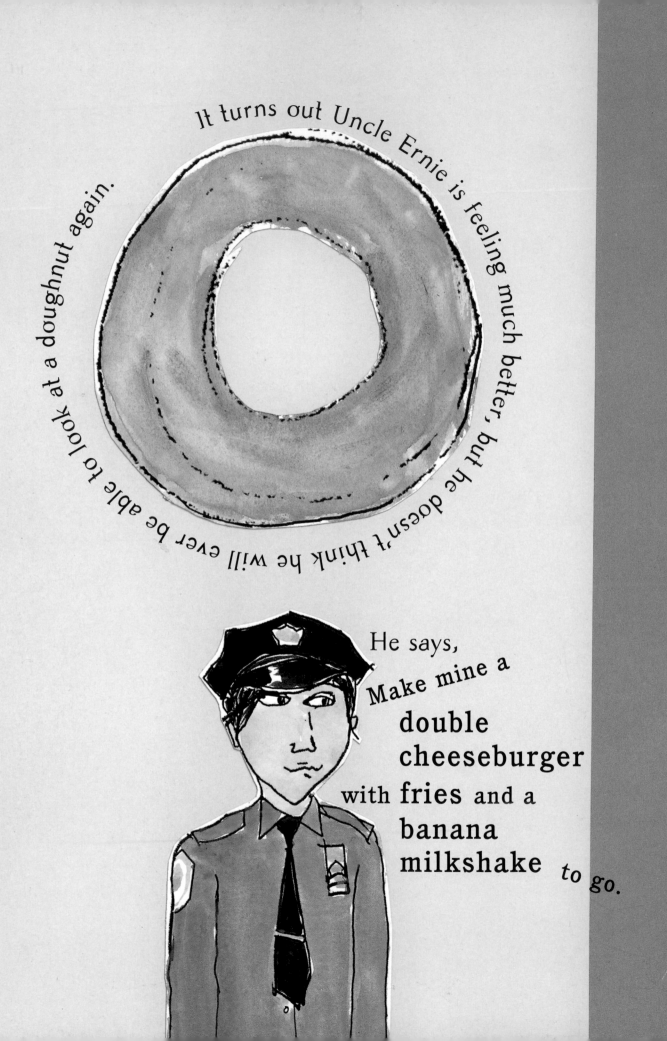

He says,

Make mine a **double cheeseburger** with **fries** and a **banana milkshake** to go.

And as for Uncle Ted, he says,
**Babysitting is the hardest job
I've ever done.**
I say, Harder than firefighting?
Uncle Ted says,
**You better
believe it,
baby.**

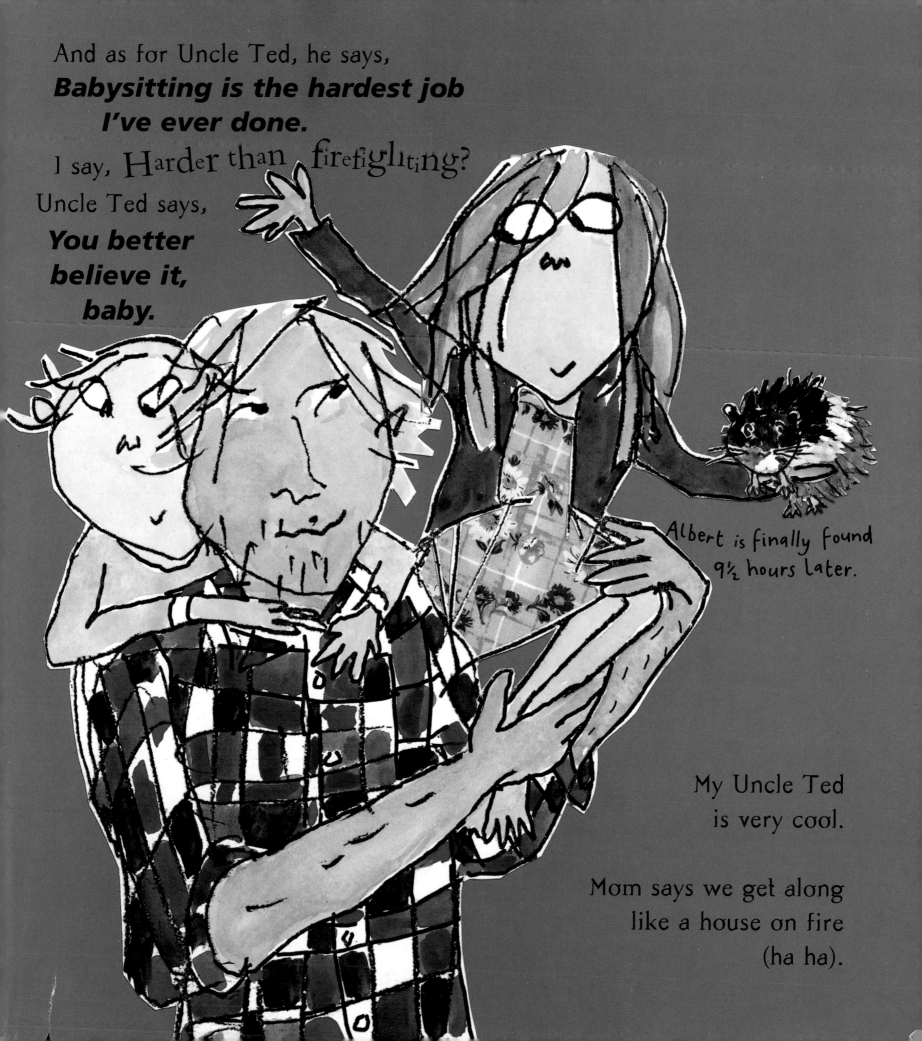

Albert is finally found
9½ hours later.

My Uncle Ted
is very cool.

Mom says we get along
like a house on fire
(ha ha).